W9-BVB-209

CORNFIELD

HIDE-AND-SEEK

BY **CHRISTINE WIDMAN** ◆ PICTURES BY **PIERR MORGAN**

MELANIE KROUPA BOOKS / FARRAR STRAUS GIROUX / NEW YORK

To my brother, Keith, and my
cousin, Doug—my favorite
cornfield hide-and-seekers.
—C.W.

For my sun-dazzling nieces and
nephews: Marquel & Teague,
Jason, Leif & Soren,
Katie & Megan, and Travis.
—P.M.

Mamaw was in the kitchen cooking butter beans. Li'l Will came running in and tugged on her apron.

"Mamaw, Mamaw. Come right now. The sun's too hot and Mattie's gone hidin'."

Mamaw wiped her hands on her apron and walked outside.

"Mattie," she called. "Where are you, boy?"

"I'm hidin', Mamaw," came a voice from the cornfield. "I'm ducked down where the dirt's damp and the corn's makin' shadows."

"Come on out now," coaxed Mamaw. "You got the chickens to feed."

"The chickens been sun-dazzled, Mamaw. They're runnin' in circles flappin' their wings."

"Mattie," said Mamaw, "I'm thinkin' *you* been sun-dazzled. Come on out and I'll make some lemonade—cold as well water— just for you."

"No," said Mattie. "The sun's too hot. I'm hidin' in the cornfield forever."

"Woo-ee," said Mamaw, fanning her face with her apron. "Li'l Will, you go fetch Grampy. Tell him Mattie's sun-dazzled."

"Mamaw, it's too hot to go runnin' for Grampy. *I* could get sun-dazzled. I'm hidin' with Mattie."

And, with a *crackly swish*, Li'l Will ran into the cornfield.

"Li'l Will, come back now," called Mamaw. "The cow needs milkin'."

"Mamaw, the cow's sun-dazzled. Got her head in the milk pail. I'm not comin' out. It's cool green in here. Me and Mattie, we're hidin' in the cornfield forever."

Mamaw paced up and down the yard. "My oh me. The sun's a-blazin', the chickens are flappin', the cow's a-lollin', my butter beans need eatin', and the kidlins are in the cornfield."

Junie May came running up.

"Mamaw, my cat's been sun-dazzled! She chased the dog into the cornfield. So I'm goin', too."

And, with a *crackly swish*, away she went.

"Come on out now, Junie May," said Mamaw, sweet-talking. "It's eatin' time soon."

"No, Mamaw, it's too hot for butter beans. The corn's kinda whisperin' and I'm cool as a frog. I'm hidin' in the cornfield forever."

"Sakes alive! Mattie
and Li'l Will and Junie May
been sun-dazzled for sure."

Mamaw ran down to the orchard. "Grampy! Grampy!"
she shouted. "The chickens are flappin', the cow's a-lollin',
my butter beans need eatin', and the kidlins are in the cornfield.
They say the sun's too hot and they're hidin' forever."

"Humph," muttered Grampy,
"the sun *is* too hot. It's cookin' my
peaches right on the trees. I'm goin'
into the cornfield with the kidlins."

And, with a *crackly swish*,
away he went.

Mamaw stared out at the cornfield. It lay before her eyes like a cool green lake under a hot yellow sun.

She walked into the kitchen.
When she came out, she was carrying
the butter beans.

"Well, kidlins," she called, "if you
gonna hide forever, guess I'll hide, too."

And, with a *swish* of her apron,
away she went.

"Mamaw?"

Mattie came running out.

"Wait, Mamaw," he said. "Here I am. I'm all cooled off."

Li'l Will came out.

"Wait, Mamaw. I got Grampy for you. Here he is."

Junie May skipped out.
"Mamaw, looky here. I found Skediddly."

"Mamaw?" said Mattie.

"Mamaw," called Li'l Will.

"Mamaw!" hollered Junie May.

Grampy said nothing because Mamaw wasn't there.
All Grampy saw was a trail of butter beans.
    "Oh no," cried all the children . . . one, two, three.
"*Mamaw's* been sun-dazzled. What'll we do?"
    "I reckon we better follow these beans," said Grampy.

Mattie, Li'l Will, Junie May, and Grampy
followed Mamaw's butter beans through the kitchen,

. . . around the chicken coop,

. . . past the barn,

. . . down to the orchard,

. . . and into the cornfield.

    There was Mamaw with the chickens, and the cow, and the dog,
and a bowl of peaches, each peach as big and rosy-pink as a summer moon.

    "Mamaw, what you doin'?"

"Ooo, kidlins, you was right," said Mamaw. "The sun's too hot and this here cornfield's as cool as dew in the mornin'. Come sit by your mamaw—you too, Grampy."

Everyone sat down under the tall green corn. The chickens
clucked, the cow mooed, the dog snuffled, and Skediddly purred.
"Have a peach," said Mamaw.

"Mmmmm," sighed all the children . . . one, two, three.

"Rrrr," snored Grampy.

 Mamaw smiled.

"My, my," she whispered, "bein' sun-dazzled sure feels sweet . . .

when you got a green cornfield to hide in."

Text copyright © 2003 by Christine Widman
Illustrations copyright © 2003 by Pierr Morgan
All rights reserved
Distributed in Canada by Douglas & McIntyre Ltd.
Color separations by Chroma Graphics PTE Ltd.
Printed and bound in China by South China Printing Company Limited
Designed by Sylvia Frezzolini Severance
First edition, 2003
10 9 8 7 6 5 4 3 2 1

Library of Congress Cataloging-in-Publication Data
Widman, Christine Barker.
    Cornfield hide-and-seek / by Christine Widman ;
illustrated by Pierr Morgan.— 1st edition
        p. cm.
    Summary: When the whole family is so hot that they hide
in the cool cornfield, Mamaw decides to play along with a
hide-and-seek game of her own.
    ISBN 0-374-31547-7
    [1. Heat—Fiction. 2. Corn—Fiction. 3. Picnicking—Fiction.
4. Farm life—Fiction. 5. Humorous stories.]   I. Morgan,
Pierr, ill. II. Title.
PZ7.W6346Co 2003
[E]—dc21
                                            2001033267